P9-DFL-590

*Poster-making party time!*

# The English Roses

# Ready, Set, Vote!

# CALLAWAY ARTS & ENTERTAINMENT

19 FULTON STREET, FIFTH FLOOR, NEW YORK, NEW YORK 10038

## PUFFIN BOOKS

Published by the Penguin Group
Penguin Young Readers Group, 345 Hudson Street, New York, New York 10014, U.S.A.
Penguin Group (Canada), 90 Eglinton Avenue East, Suite 700, Toronto, Ontario,
Canada M4P2Y3 (a division of Pearson Penguin Canada Inc.)

Penguin Books Ltd., Registered Offices: 80 Strand, London WC2R 0RL, England

First published in the United States of America by Callaway Arts & Entertainment and Puffin Books, 2009

1   3   5   7   9   10   8   6   4   2

First Edition

Produced by Callaway Arts & Entertainment
Nicholas Callaway, President and Publisher
John Lee, CEO
Cathy Ferrara, Managing Editor and Production Director
Toshiya Masuda, Art Director
Nelson Gómez, Director of Digital Technology
Amy Cloud, Senior Editor
Bomina Kim, Design Assistant
Ivan Wong, Jr. and José Rodríguez, Production
Jennifer Caffrey, Executive Assistant

Special thanks to Doug Whiteman and Mariann Donato.

Puffin Books ISBN 978-0-14-241127-8

Printed in the United States of America

www.madonna.com     www.callaway.com     www.penguin.com/youngreaders

All of Madonna's proceeds from this book will be donated to
Raising Malawi (www.raisingmalawi.org), an orphan-care initiative.

# The English Roses

## by Madonna

### With Rebecca Gómez

## Ready, Set, Vote!

PUFFIN

CALLAWAY

New York
2009

illustrated by
Jeffrey Fulvimari

Book 10

# Contents

# CHAPTER I

# Three-Eyed Eels

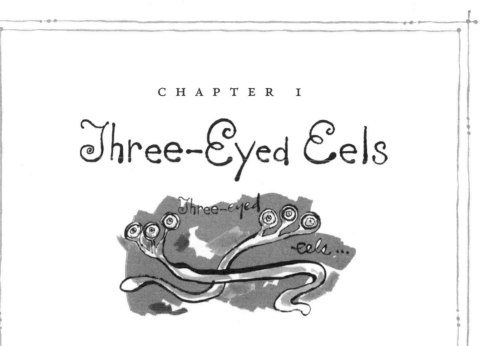

N ow, if you'll remember, when last we
left the English Roses, they were . . .
What's that?

I must be losing my hearing,
because it sounded like you said you
don't know about the English Roses! You are
kidding, right? First of all, it's not a "what"; they're a
"who"! You know, the five fabulous friends? Together

through anything? BFF forever? Is any of this ringing a bell for you?

Oh, come on! There can be only one possible excuse for this shocking lack of knowledge on your part. Your parents took you on a scientific excursion, didn't they? What were you, submerged several miles under the Arctic ice cap doing research on bottom-dwelling ocean creatures? I hope that research was worth it. I hope you found your fill of three-eyed eels or nine-legged octopuses or whatever.

Based in London, the English Roses are sixth graders at Hampstead School. They are five best friends: Binah Rossi, Charlotte Ginsberg, Amy Brook, Grace Harrison, and Nicole Rissman. I can guess what you may be thinking: best friends are a two-for. On the rare occasion, a trio. But a quintet? Trust me, in this case the five best friends are five best friends. And they're fabulous. But more important than their fabulousity (yes, something is more important than being fabulous) is the strength of their friendship. These are five girls who would do anything for one another: fight any fight, weather any storm, dance any dance, suffer any sale . . . You get the picture. Nowhere that I'm aware in the annals of humanity has there ever existed a friendship like this.

Now that we've got you up to speed, you can sit back, relax, and enjoy the latest escapade in the Roses' lives. Hold on tight; it's a doozy!

BINAH!  CHARLOTTE!  Grace!  NICOLE!  amy!

ALL CLEAR ???

CHAPTER 2

# Girl Down!

( the sound of SPRING getting ) SPRUNG

So, as I was saying (or trying to, anyway, before you brought up all those slimy three-eyed eels!), spring had finally sprung. Gone were the gray and gloomy days of a London late winter. The cold north winds had put up a valiant fight, but warm breezes from southern

France and Italy had won the day. A cheery sun was peeping out from behind fluffy clouds as the English Roses made their way out of school.

"I just saw a cardinal!" Binah called.

"I do love the spring." Amy sighed.

"Me, too," Binah added. "It's so lovely and warm, and the flowers are blooming."

"And we can finally play football outside!" Grace cheered. (Note to American readers: football = soccer. Please remember, this story takes place on another continent.)

"Actually," continued Amy, "I was mostly thinking about my closet full of fantastic spring fashions."

"You and your clothes!" Grace teased her.

"You and your football!" Amy teased her right back.

"You know, ladies—" Binah began.

"We know!" Charlotte chimed in. "One girl's passion—"

"Is another girl's nightmare!" Nicole finished the quote. It was one of the Roses' favorite quotes, coming as it did from their favorite teacher of all time: Miss Fluffernutter.

Miss Fluffernutter? Oh, don't get me started. We haven't got time for that now. Just know that she taught the Roses way back in fifth grade, but their love for her is just as strong now as it was then. She is a teeny bit odd, but mostly loving and cheerful and kind. In her heart, each girl would like to grow up to be a lot like Miss Fluffernutter. Without the teeny odd part. And with better fashion sense (in Amy's view). And with neater hair (in each girl's view). Didn't I tell you not to get me started?!

Back to the girls, leaving school on a just-barely warm and slightly sunny early spring day.

"I can't believe that we have no homework," Nicole said. If you detect the slightest bit of regret in that remark, you're not imagining things. Nicole loves school. Even now she was pulling her journal from her shoulder bag and idly flipping through the pages.

"Let's just enjoy the afternoon," Grace said. "I'm so happy to be out of that stinky building." As she spoke she pulled an ever-present ball from her backpack. She began to dribble the ball expertly from one foot to another.

"Speaking of odor," Amy said as she tucked an errant red curl back behind her ear, "is it just me or do the hallways seem really messy?"

"You know," Binah answered, "I'm not one to complain, but the bathrooms were rather dirty today."

"Dirty?" snorted Charlotte, smoothing an imaginary wrinkle from her silk skirt. "They are revolting!"

"And how about lunch?" asked Grace. "My fish and chips (note to American readers: chips = French fries, 'kay?) were practically inedible."

The girls were silent for approximately forty-two seconds as they thought about school. The only sound was the smack, whack of the ball passing from one of Grace's nimble feet to the other.

"Maybe the janitors and lunch servers caught spring fever?" suggested Nicole.

"Adults don't get spring fever!" Amy declared.

"Only kids. Right?" She pushed her floral Hèrmes headband back on her head and looked at her friends for confirmation.

"I don't know," Binah said slowly. "Things do seem to be slipping around Hampstead."

"Well, what can we do?" asked Grace as she jogged after the ball, which had skittered around the corner of the school building.

The sun's rays picked out golden highlights in Binah's hair as she answered. "I don't know, but there must be something. My dad always says that we shouldn't complain about things—"

"We should try and change them!" Charlotte finished for her. "My mum always says that, too."

"It must be in the parenting handbook," Amy noted, "because I've heard it plenty of times, too!"

*CRASH!*

"Oww!"

"Grace!" Amy, Nicole, Binah, and Charlotte all cried at once. They rushed around the corner of the building to find Grace, a large rubbish bin, a spilled book bag, and a still-rolling ball. There had been a clash between Grace and the rubbish bin, and the rubbish bin had won.

"My foot!" Grace cried as she cradled her foot, sniffing back tears.

# CHAPTER 3

# The State of Grace

"What happened, Grace?" Charlotte cried as she rushed to her fallen friend's side.

"I'll run back inside for some ice," Binah said, ever practical. "The rest of you should keep her from moving."

"Yes," Nicole agreed. "We need to find out what got hurt."

"*I* got hurt!" Grace choked out, trying not to cry. "I was running after the ball when I smashed into the bin. I didn't even see it there."

"Can you wiggle your toes, Grace?" Amy asked. "I think you can tell if anything is broken by wiggling your toes. If you can wiggle, nothing's broken."

"Broken!" Grace cried. "I can't break anything; I've got football practice starting the day after tomorrow!"

"Wiggle, Grace, wiggle," the girls urged.

Under their watchful eyes, Grace gave her toes a tentative wiggle. The other girls could see slight movement under the dirty toes of her worn sneaker.

"I can move my toes!" Grace announced triumphantly. "It hurts, but I can move them."

There was a sudden commotion behind them. The girls turned to see Miss Fluffernutter approaching, with Binah scurrying along behind her.

"Oh my! Oh my!" Miss Flutternutter repeated over and over. "Whatever has happened, Grace?" She knelt at Grace's side and placed an ice pack on Grace's injured foot.

Binah explained to the other Roses, "I was on my way to the nurse's office when I passed Miss Fluffernutter in the hallway. She asked me what was wrong; and when I told her what had happened, she

23

told me she was the perfect person for the job because of her first aid training."

"Yes, extensive training, yes," Miss Flutternutter said as she gently prodded Grace's ankle. Carefully removing Grace's sneaker, she continued her examination. She paused for a moment and frowned. "Although, I guess you don't technically need CPR, do you?"

"No!" Grace cried.

OH MY, OH MY.!!!

"Yes, well, I was at the top of my certification class," Miss Fluffernutter announced proudly.

"Certification class?" Amy asked.

"All Hampstead teachers need to be Red Cross certified, don't you know?" answered Miss Fluffernutter. "And I was almost the best student in the class. Well, I would have been except that my hair kept blowing over the dummy's mouth."

"Who's a dummy?" Charlotte asked, confused.

"No, no, no one is a dummy. Well, certainly some people aren't quite as smart as we would hope. But that's neither here nor there," Miss Fluffernutter continued. "We were using a first aid dummy to practice CPR. My hair kept falling out of its lovely bun and covering the dummy's mouth. Very difficult to administer CPR that way, I can assure you!"

Trying to get Miss Fluffernutter onto a perhaps less-confusing topic, Binah asked her about the dirty school. "Has something happened to the school budget, Miss Fluffernutter?"

"Hmm. What? The budget? Oh no, dear. Not that I know of. Why do you ask?"

Nicole realized what Binah was trying to do and quickly chimed in. "It's just that, you know, things seem to be getting rundown. Why, just yesterday the pencil sharpeners in three different class-rooms—and the library!—were broken."

This reminded Grace of lunch. With a giant sniff, she added, "And my lunch was practically inedible today."

"Now, girls—" Miss Fluffernutter started.

Grace interrupted, "And the rubbish bins, Miss Fluffernutter! If this can had been where it belonged, I never would have crashed into it!" Grace pointed dramatically at the offending object,

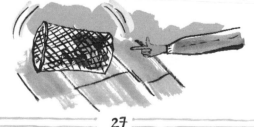

which rolled lazily across the blacktop away from them.

Miss Fluffernutter carefully re-laced Grace's sneaker and stood to look at the girls. Her expression mirrored her concern. This was just one of the many reasons the Roses loved Miss Fluffernutter so absolutely. While another teacher may have pooh-poohed their complaints, Miss Fluffernutter took them seriously.

"Hmm," she said again. She reached down a hand to help Grace to her feet. Grace tentatively stood and carefully placed her weight on the injured foot. Binah started the round of applause for Grace's heroism. Grace took one tentative step. Then another. She had a definite limp, but she was moving.

"Yeah, Grace!" the girls called. "You go, girl!"

"Well, ladies," Miss Fluffernutter started, "first of all, how are we going to get Grace home? She cannot go far on that injured foot."

"That's no problem, Miss Fluffernutter," Charlotte said as she quickly took out her cell phone. "I will ask our driver, Royston, to pick us up."

"Wonderful, Charlotte. Thank you," Miss Fluffernutter said warmly. To Grace she said, "You won't be running around on that foot anytime soon, Grace."

"But Miss Fluffernutter!" Grace tried to complain. "Practice starts this week!"

Miss Fluffernutter patted Grace's arm consolingly. "I am sorry, my dear. I'm not a doctor, but I do know that running around the football field could cause you a lot of harm."

"Lucky for you your dad's a doctor, Grace!" Amy tried to cheer up her friend. Grace only scowled.

A group of students, curious about what was happening, drifted over from the school doorway.

"Off you go, now." Miss Fluffernutter shooed them away. "Nothing to see here!"

Once Charlotte had completed her call, Miss Fluffernutter continued. "On another topic, I don't know that anything has changed at Hampstead School. I hadn't actually noticed any difference. But, if something is bothering you girls, you know what to do?"

"We've got it, Miss Fluffernutter!" Binah said. "If we don't like it—"

Amy completed the quote. "We must work to change it."

Miss Fluffernutter smiled proudly at the girls. "You really are the most extraordinary students!"

And that was another thing about Miss Fluffernutter. In addition to being warmhearted, she somehow made you feel that *you* were kind, warmhearted, and brilliant—even if you were feeling mean, petty, and silly. She could see the better part of you even when you couldn't see it!

A car horn tooted from the street, and the group saw Royston pulling up at the gate. Before anyone could take a step, Nicole startled them with a cry. "Hold on, everyone, I have the most brill idea!"

*Spring has sprung in London!*

CHAPTER 4

# Hats in the Ring!

O nly after Royston had tucked them all safely into the backseat of the car and they'd said good-bye to Miss Fluffernutter would Nicole share her idea with them. With their teacher's cries of "Take good care of Grace!" still echoing in their ears, they pestered Nicole.

"What's the big idea, Nicole?" Grace asked.

"Well," Nicole answered, "as Miss Fluffernutter was helping Grace, I saw the rubbish bin rolling across the yard. That reminded me of the dirty bathrooms. The dirty bathrooms reminded me of the pencil sharpeners. The pencil sharpeners reminded me of the library. When I was there yesterday after school, there was a second grader trying to do homework. She kept asking Mrs. Souza for help. But Mrs. Souza is the librarian, and she doesn't have time to help with homework. I was trying to help the girl, but—"

"Nicole!" Amy warned her friend. "Your idea?"

"Oh yes. Sorry!" Nicole said. "So, back to the rubbish bin; we've all said that things seem to be slipping at Hampstead, right?"

"Right!" her friends chorused.

"We all agree that we must get involved, right?" Nicole asked.

"Right, again!" the Roses answered her.

"Remember when Miss Fluffernutter sent away that group of students who were trying to gawk at Grace?" Nicole asked. "Did anyone else notice what Emma Harms was wearing?"

"No!" answered Amy, Charlotte, Grace, and Binah, almost as one.

"She was wearing a pin!" Nicole answered.

"So what?" Charlotte asked. "Pins are big this season."

"Not a jewelry pin," Nicole said. "A vote pin. Student elections are coming up, you know." Nicole continued. "Whoever is elected student body president this spring will take office in the fall, at the start of the new school year." (The thought of a new school year made Nicole smile, even as it made the other Roses shudder!)

"Yes?" prompted Amy.

Nicole suddenly seemed a bit shy. "Well," she started, then seemed unable to go on. She took a deep breath. "I thought perhaps I could run for president. Then we could really work to change things around Hampstead. What do you think?"

There was a brief moment of silence. Then the backseat erupted in noise. It's truly a wonder that Royston didn't simply drive right off the road. I mean, the noise was that sudden and explosive. It wasn't a bad noise; it was the babble of five girls talking excitedly . . . all at once.

"Why, that's fantastic!"

"You go, Nikki!"

"We're on board!"

"English Roses Rule!"

This last one came from Grace, who simply couldn't suppress her competitive spirit.

"You really think I could do it?" Nicole asked her friends.

"Oh, Nicole," said Binah, "you can totally do it. And you'd do a fantastic job, too."

"This is great, Nicole," Grace said. "With you in power, we'd be certain to get new sports uniforms!"

"Or sushi in the cafeteria!" Charlotte chimed in.

"I'm thinking of a class on fashion design," Amy said hopefully.

"We should get a bigger cage for Ernest, maybe with some new hamster toys," Binah added.

"I was thinking more about homework help centers, cleaner hallways, community outreach programs—things like that," Nicole said. "But I'm really glad to see that you guys are enthusiastic!"

"I just know you're going to win, Nicole," Binah said loyally.

"How can we help?" Charlotte asked her friend.

"Well," Nicole said thoughtfully, "I guess I'll need to figure out what I really want to change about Hampstead. Those will be my issues."

"Oh! You've definitely got issues!" laughed Grace.

"Very funny!" Nicole laughed. "Then I'll need posters. . . ." Her voice trailed off, and she seemed lost in thought.

"I know exactly what you

Toys

cage

need!" Charlotte cried. "You'll need a campaign manager. I nominate Grace for the job!"

"Me?" Grace gulped.

"Yes," Binah said. "That's a wonderful idea. You're so clever, Grace."

"It's not her cleverness I'm after," said Charlotte. "It's her quick thinking. When Hampstead is down 3-1 in the fourth period—or is it quarter"—Grace couldn't help but smile and roll her eyes—"who do you want running with the ball?"

"Grace!" Nicole said.

"First of all," Grace began, "it's a quarter in football, not a period!"

"Anyway, Grace," Binah interjected, "you heard what Miss Fluffernutter said: You're going to need to rest your

foot. That means you can't start practice this week."

"I don't know. . . ." Grace said doubtfully.

"Oh, come on, Grace!" Charlotte said. "You'd be a great help to Nikki."

"You sure would, Grace!" Nicole said. "I need you on my side!"

Grace gave Nicole a high five and then declared, "I'll do it, Nicole. Together we'll slaughter the competition!"

A bit taken aback, Nicole glanced at the other Roses and rolled her eyes. That Grace!

CHAPTER 5

# Full Steam Ahead

The next morning at school, Grace appeared on crutches with a bandage wrapped around her foot.

"My dad says it's just a bad bruise," she explained to her friends. "I've got to be off it for a few weeks."

"I'm sorry about your foot, Grace," Nicole said, "but that gives us just enough time to get my campaign in gear. Elections are next week!"

"Who are we up against?" Charlotte wondered.

"I have good news and bad news," Nicole answered. "I stopped by the principal's office this morning to officially register as a candidate. The good news is that there is only one other candidate for president."

"And the bad news?" wondered Binah.

"The bad news is that my opponent is . . . Fanny Kingsbury," Nicole announced.

"Yuck!" said Charlotte.

"How unpleasant," said Binah.

Now, you may be wondering why the name Fanny Kingsbury caused such a stir among the Roses, and I'm perfectly happy to explain. Fanny was . . . hmmm, how to say this? You know when someone says something that's just a tiny bit mean?

Just a tad snarky? You hear it and you're not sure if you should be hurt or offended or angry? She'd once said to Binah, in front of all the other Roses, "Binah, I just love your style. You have a way of making quite a great outfit from really inferior pieces." Honestly, how are you supposed to react to that? Is she insulting you for having poor-quality clothing? Or is she truly complimenting your style? Well, Fanny was the master of comments such as that. If there ever was a competition for slightly off remarks, Fanny would win it hands down. Hopefully, that would be the only thing Fanny would win. After all, Nicole's the one we are rooting for!

"Don't worry, Nicole," said Grace. "We'll crush her!"

"I don't want to actually crush her, Grace," Nicole said a bit nervously. "I just want to win the election."

"Oh, don't worry," Grace said confidently. "You're going to win this election. We're unstoppable, right Roses?"

As Charlotte, Binah, and Amy nodded, Nicole forced a weak smile, and Grace continued, "What we need is a strategy, right?"

"Yes," Nicole agreed.

"Last night, since I couldn't practice anyway, I drew up a little plan," Grace announced as she pulled four crumpled pieces of notepaper from her backpack. She asked Amy to turn around and then proceeded to straighten and smooth the papers on Amy's back.

"Careful!" Amy warned. "This jacket is from Stella McCartney's boutique!"

"It's lovely, Amy," Binah said. And it was. Amy wouldn't leave the house unless she was camera ready. You never knew when your photo might be

snapped, right? Everyone knew that London was simply crawling with paparazzi. You know, the photographers who jump out from behind parked cars to take pictures of celebrities looking awful? The awfuller, the better?

"Okay, here we go," Grace said. "This is the war plan." And there it was, on four sheets of Grace's special "I Get My Kicks from Football!" notepad: an involved list of directions. The Roses could see items such as Pep Rally, PA Announcements, Poster Party, and Button Bonanza.

"I don't know if we can do all of this stuff," Grace said, "but this should get us off to a great start."

"Wow, Grace!" Nicole exclaimed. "Look at all the work you've done. This is wonderful!"

"As I said," Grace answered, "I was so bored last

night; I couldn't even kick the ball around! So I started thinking about your campaign and what we can do to get you into that office, Nikki."

"With this list, you're sure to win, Nicole!" said Charlotte. "Where should we start?"

"Posters!" Grace answered. "We've got to announce Nicole's candidacy, and I think posters are the best way to go."

"Shall we go to my house after school?" Charlotte asked. "Royston can pick us up, Nigella will make us snacks (yes, yes, Charlotte's family has a cook, too. I know, I know; but don't be a hater!), and we've got lots of supplies."

"I'm in!" said Amy.

"I'm sure it will be okay with my dad," Binah said. "I'll just call him from your house."

"Thank you, Roses!" Nicole said. "With you all on my side, how can I lose?"

"Oh, don't worry, Nicole," Grace said seriously. "Fanny will never know what hit her! We'll make her sorry that she ever decided to run against you!"

"Oh, Grace," Nicole began, "I don't think she decided to run against me, I think she just—"

But Grace was already swinging away on her crutches, calling to a group of friends from her football team, "Hey! You all! You need to know that Nicole Rissman is running for president, and she's the only candidate worth voting for!"

Nicole gulped and looked after her campaign manager. The other Roses looked at one another uneasily. Was Grace perhaps taking this whole election a tiny bit too seriously?

CHAPTER 6

# Politics As Usual

"Hey, Binah! Over here!" Charlotte called from the backseat of her family's Rolls Royce. All of the Roses except for Binah were already in the car. As Binah made her way over to the car, parked at the curb, the other girls were discussing what they'd need for their poster party.

"I'll make sugar cookies," Charlotte said.

"I'll make croissants," Nicole offered.

"Oh, Nicole," teased Amy, "you're so French!"

"Well, I was born in Paris, you know!" Nicole teased.

Binah climbed in, and Royston gently closed the back door. "That was odd," Binah noted, almost to herself, as Royston smoothly steered the car into traffic.

"What was odd?" Amy asked her.

"I was going to call my dad from your house, Charlotte," Binah answered. "I wanted to make sure it was okay for me to stay for a while. I'd made a shepherd's pie for tonight's dinner, so all he'll need to do is heat it up." (It's no secret that Binah does an awful lot around the house. Binah's mother died when she was quite young; and for almost as long as Binah can remember, it's been just her and her dad. No worries, though, they're quite a team!) "On my way out of the building, I passed Miss Fluffernutter's room. . . ."

"And?" Grace prompted.

"I started to say good-bye to her," Binah went on, "but she said she would walk with me. She said that she had plans to see my dad after school!"

"Are you in trouble, Binah?" asked Amy.

"As if!" snorted Charlotte.

"No, I'm not in any kind of trouble," Binah said. "Miss Fluffernutter seemed surprised that I didn't know that she and my dad were having coffee after school."

"Well, that's all right, then," Grace said. "There's nothing wrong with them having coffee, is there?"

"No way!" said Amy.

"I think it's lovely," offered Nicole.

"Yes . . ." said Binah.

Suddenly, the same image appeared in the minds of each of the English Roses. At a recent skating party, none of them had missed the sight of Binah's dad, Mr. Rossi, skating hand in hand with Miss Fluffernutter. And each girl, even Grace, couldn't help feeling a tiny thrill about the possibility of romance in the air. Mr. Rossi and Miss Fluffernutter? What a fantastic pairing. How lucky Binah would be!

But this is not a story about Mr. Rossi and Miss Fluffernutter! This is the story of Nicole's bid for class presidency, so let's get back to that!

The girls spent a lovely afternoon making all sorts of posters in support of Nicole. Nicole shared with them all of her ideas. She wanted to organize a homework center, in which older students could volunteer to help younger students. She wanted to organize a Community Outreach Committee, which would help coordinate volunteers for projects in the neighborhood around Hampstead School. She wanted expanded library hours. She also wanted a cleaner school.

"I have a question, Nikki," Amy said. "I understand everything except for the cleaner school bit. We can't force the cleaning people to work longer hours. Is there anything we can do to have a cleaner school?"

"That's a good question," Nicole agreed.

"Maybe we could have prizes?" Binah suggested. "Maybe Principal Turvey would allow a school-wide contest. The classroom judged the cleanest would get a homework pass or extra recess time or something."

"That's a great idea!" Grace said. "Everyone loves a competition, right?"

"I also want some fun in my platform," Nicole noted. "How about a pizza party on Friday afternoons? Or maybe an ice cream option in the cafeteria?"

"That sounds wonderful, Nicole," Amy said. "Who wouldn't like pizza or ice cream?"

"No one," Grace said firmly. "So Nicole's platform, or goals, are to improve life around the school. And have fun. How can we work that into the campaign?"

"I saw some kids with 'Fanny First' buttons," Binah said. "That sounds a little strange, if you ask me! How about if we make some 'Rissman Rules' buttons?"

"What about 'Help Hampstead'?" Charlotte offered.

"I love that idea!" Nicole said. "We can make a difference and have a good time while we do it!"

As they listened to Nicole talk so passionately about her ideas, the other Roses were even prouder of their friend than before. Nicole's purpose was pure, and she truly wanted to help her fellow students. Which made what happened at school the next day all the more upsetting!

It seems that Fanny Kingsbury's team had caught the poster bug first. When the Roses walked into school the following morning, there were posters asking students to make "Fanny First" all over the hallways. That in and of itself wasn't so bad. After all, each candidate is allowed to advertise, right?

What was upsetting was what some of the posters implied. Remember we discussed how Fanny was very good at snarky comments? And remember that Nicole was born in Paris? As you are well aware, Paris is not in England; Paris is in France. Nicole is a British citizen because her parents are British citizens. All clear? Well, that was not so clear in Fanny's posters. Some of them told voters to vote for the candidate who was "truly" British.

Some of them urged voters to select the candidate whose first language is English. Now, Nicole's first language is English, but she is fluent in French.

"Oh my gosh!" Nicole gasped when she saw the posters.

"But these are lies!" Binah cried.

"This is horrible!" Grace exclaimed. "Who does she think she is, the queen of England?"

"How could she do this?" asked Amy.

Charlotte narrowed her eyes and studied one

offending poster. "Technically, she's not lying," she finally said.

"What?!" Nicole shouted. "Are you agreeing with her, Charlotte?"

"Of course not!" Charlotte answered. "But you'll notice that she was very clever with the way she wrote the posters. She never actually accuses you of anything."

"It's not very nice," Binah said.

"No, it's not." Grace agreed. "And look at her poster! She's promising all sorts of impossible things!"

"Oh, this is crazy!" Charlotte said. "She says she's going to get us soda machines in the cafeteria."

"And no homework, ever, on Fridays!" Amy read.

*Nicole and Fanny in the election ring*

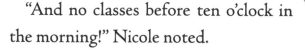

"And no classes before ten o'clock in the morning!" Nicole noted.

"It's all nonsense," Grace told them. "If Fanny-British-to-her-core thinks this will work, she's nuts! But don't worry, I'm on this."

With that, Grace stalked off down the hallway . . . as well as anyone on crutches can stalk. Nicole looked devastated.

"Don't worry, Nicole," Amy said. "We made beautiful posters, and we're going to put them up."

"Yes," said Binah. "By the time we're done, everyone in school will know how wonderful your ideas are, Nikki."

With that, the four Roses (minus Grace) worked as quickly as possible to put up their posters before the first bell rang. When that bell did shrill through the hallways, the Roses paused to examine their handiwork. They had covered many walls with posters. There could be no doubt, to quote Grace, the Game Was On!

P.S. Although this is most emphatically *not* a story about Mr. Rossi and Miss Fluffernutter, you

are normal red-blooded readers, are you not? As such, I am quite sure that you're very curious about their coffee situation. When Binah arrived home after the marathon poster-making session, she found Mr. Rossi and Miss Fluffernutter sitting cozily close together on the living-room sofa. They were talking and laughing, surrounded by empty coffee mugs, napkins, and plates. Miss Fluffernutter left soon after Binah arrived home, but not before giving Binah a big hug and wishing her a happy evening. Mr. Rossi was more talkative than usual during dinner (the shepherd's pie was delicious!) and Binah's spirits were light, indeed, by the time she'd finished her homework and headed to bed. That night she dreamed of fairy cakes and garden parties—dreams full of laughter and love.

CHAPTER 7

# Is That Fair?

After the poster incident, school that morning went very smoothly. Many students went out of their way to tell Nicole how happy they were that she'd joined the race. It seems that more than one person had been at the receiving end of one of Fanny's barbed comments! Nicole made sure to thank each person warmly. Whenever possible she, or one of the other Roses, addressed the . . . innuendos . . . of Fanny's election posters. They explained over and over again that Nicole was, in fact, a British citizen. The Roses talked about Nicole's plans for the school; most students were lukewarm about the home-work help center (*What is wrong with people?* Nicole couldn't help but wonder) but happy about the thought of cleaner hallways and bathrooms. By the time recess rolled around, Nicole was feeling very good about her chances of winning.

Picture, if you will, the five best friends sitting at a picnic table at lunchtime. They were minding their own business. They were not asking for trouble. Which didn't seem to bother Fanny Kingsbury. She sauntered by and asked, seemingly innocently,

"Did you have French fries with lunch, Nicole?"

"I'm sorry, Fanny, what did you say?" Nicole asked.

"Oh! I guess maybe you didn't understand me? I was speaking English, after all," Fanny said.

"What's your point, Fanny?" Grace asked impatiently.

"Oh, no point, really," Fanny answered innocently. "My campaign manager, Alexis Leeds—as in Leeds, England—and I were wondering about Nicole's lunch."

Short detour: What do you need to know about Alexis Leeds? In a nutshell: she's the school's self-appointed journalist with a penchant for gossip. Like Fanny, she doesn't try to be a bad person. But, like Fanny, sometimes she veers ever so slightly into Bad Territory. The Roses had had a slight dustup with her earlier in the year when she printed some not-so-true things about Nicole and a boy who was her friend. But you remember that, right?

"Why do you want to know about her lunch?" Binah asked.

"We're just curious about what her type of person eats," Alexis answered smoothly.

"And what type is that?" Grace asked. The other Roses glanced at one another nervously. Grace was growing impatient with Fanny and Alexis. Even if they didn't recognize the warning signs, the Roses did. You did not want to make Grace angry.

Alexis Leeds

Back in Action

"You know," Fanny answered. "People who aren't from here."

"Listen, Queen Mum!" Grace said loudly. "You're spreading a bunch of lies, and you know it!"

"Grace!" Charlotte raised her own voice.

"Calm down, everyone," Nicole said.

"We'll calm down," Fanny said angrily. "As soon as you make your campaign manager say she's sorry!"

"Sorry for what?" Grace asked indignantly as she got to her feet and moved her crutches into position. "Why would I apologize to you? You're the ones who lied!"

"No, we didn't!" Alexis answered.

"Yes, you did!" Grace roared back.

Nicole knew she had to act quickly. Other students were

H.R.H. Queen Fanny I

noticing the commotion and coming over to see what was happening. She gently touched Fanny's arm. While she was doing that, Charlotte put an arm around Grace's shoulders and carefully moved her away from the table.

"As your campaign manager," Grace began, "I have a problem with the posters that Fanny and her people have put up. She's telling lies about you, and I don't like it."

"We didn't lie!" yelped Alexis.

"Her posters imply that you shouldn't be elected because you weren't born here. They say that you speak another language. That you're not fit to be president!" Grace cried to Nicole.

"Some of those things are true, Grace, and some are not," Nicole answered. "But this is a free country, and people have a right to say what they want about me."

Charlotte looked at the crowd of students now tensely gathered around. She nodded and said, "All right; we're through here. See you all inside." With that, the English Roses gathered around Grace and began herding her back to the school.

Angrily, Grace asked Nicole, "How can you let them say those things about you?"

"They can say whatever they want," Binah

reminded Grace. "We know what is true and not true."

"And most students know the truth," said Charlotte.

"It does seem to me that Fanny and her gang are not fighting fair," said Amy.

"I'll say! Is she a member of the royal family and we didn't know it?" Grace asked sarcastically.

"But," Nicole said, "this is my campaign, Grace. You are helping me to run it, but I'm the one running for president. I need to do this on my own terms."

"What terms?" asked Grace. "Right now I want to sweep the floor with Fanny Queensbury!"

"Decent terms," said Nicole. "Honorable terms. If I have to cheat to win, then I don't want to win.

Fanny and Alexis can say whatever they want, but I know who I am."

"And we know who you are!" chorused the other Roses. "And we love you just the way you are."

"Who could not love you?" asked Amy.

"It really doesn't matter if people love me or not," said Nicole. "I've been giving this a lot of

thought. I honestly think that I would make a very good president. I know that I can do a great job if I am given the chance. I'll work hard and do what's best for other students.  I'm not going to call people names or get into fights; I'm just going to tell the voters my positions and let them decide."

"Three cheers for Nicole!" Charlotte called as they entered the school.

"Rissman, Rissman, she's our wo-man!" shouted Amy.

As the girls walked into their classroom, Nicole pulled Grace over to the side.

"I appreciate what you're trying to do, Grace," she told her friend. "I know you want me to win. I want me to win! But we need to be fair."

"But—" Grace interrupted.

"Yes, Grace," Nicole continued. "I know Fanny may not always play by the rules. But that's okay. That's her choice. I have to live with myself, and I have to be proud of myself. I think we can win this election fair and square. Are you with me?"

"Yes!" Grace answered her friend, but her mind was far away. Dangerously far away.

CHAPTER 8

# Grace on the Warpath

The next few days passed smoothly at Hampstead. Over the weekend, the English Roses made a bunch of campaign buttons, which they passed out the following Monday. It was great fun for Nicole to walk down the hallways and see other students wearing buttons with her slogan on them: Rissman

Rules! With the election itself planned for the end of the week, the Roses were sure Nicole would win. Fanny had many supporters and the race appeared to be pretty tight, but, still, the girls were optimistic.

And that's what always gets us into trouble, isn't it? I don't mean to say that optimism is a bad thing—not at all. Optimism is lovely and helpful and gets us out of bed in the morning. I'm also not saying that Nicole was overconfident, because she wasn't—not at all. What I'm saying is that Fanny was Fanny. And people like Fanny aren't content to let things play themselves out. She wanted to win the election, and she didn't mind venturing oh-so-slightly into Bad Territory to do so. Watch out! Here come those three-eyed eels again!

The Thursday before the election was rainy and dreary. The Roses shivered as they hoisted umbrellas over their heads on their way into school. As they rushed through the hallways, something seemed off. It wasn't until they'd paused in front of Mrs. Moss's classroom that they noticed what was different. The walls were still plastered with posters urging students to vote for Nicole or Fanny. But some of Fanny's posters looked a little different. Someone had made slight changes to them!

In one she now appeared to be the queen. Someone had taped a homemade paper crown on top of her head. In another, she appeared to be a barrister of the court, with a puffy white wig over her own hair. In yet another, someone had taped a speech bubble next to her mouth. The bubble said, "By my royal decree: Homework is banned from Hampstead School!"

Almost as soon as they noticed the vandalism, Nicole heard herself being paged over the public address system. "Nicole Rissman, please report to the principal's office immediately."

Nicole's face went white as she faced her friends. "I've never been to the principal's office before!" she cried. "I think I'm in big trouble! Who could have done something like this?"

"There's been a terrible mistake, Nikki!" Binah tried to comfort her frightened friend.

"I'll walk with you," Charlotte offered.

Grace was silent. As Nicole and Charlotte hurried off down the hallway, Grace called out, "I'll tell Mrs. Moss where you are, Nicole." Binah and Amy couldn't help but notice the tiny smile playing around the corners of her mouth.

Poor Nicole! I'm not calling her a Goody Two-shoes; I would never do that. I will say, however, that not even the principal believed that she was behind the poster mess. The fact remained, though, that Fanny's posters had been altered, while Nicole's remained untouched. What to do? There wasn't time for Fanny to make a whole new batch of posters, so Principal Turvey decided that all the posters would have to be taken down. He asked Nicole to spend her lunch hour and study break periods taking down all the election posters. As they trudged back to Mrs. Moss's room, Nicole and Charlotte could only wonder who was behind the vandalism.

"Who could have done this?" Nicole asked herself, half aloud.

PRincipal TuRVey

not so → happy

"I don't know, Nikki," Charlotte answered. "But try not to worry; everyone knows you would never be so spiteful."

But maybe Charlotte was wrong. Maybe other students thought Nicole really was responsible. As the two girls walked into their classroom, they were greeted with silence. Nicole couldn't be sure, but it seemed as though the other students were looking at her differently. Suspiciously. She didn't like it, not one bit.

And this is why the Roses spent their afternoon study period in the hallways. It was not fun, but in typical fashion, the Roses pulled together. Almost before they knew it, they'd filled four big bags with crumpled poster paper and bits of tape.

"What would I do without you all?" Nicole

asked as she gazed at her friends. "This would have taken me forever to do by myself!"

"Why would you ever think of doing this by yourself?" Charlotte asked. "That's why we're here!"

"I think Fanny got what she deserved!" Grace announced.

"Grace!" Binah exclaimed, a little bit shocked. "Don't you think you're being hard on Fanny?"

"No; I think she had it coming to her. No one picks on Nicole and gets away with it!" Grace answered fiercely.

"We know that she can be mean, and I don't like it one bit, but we can't stoop to her level!" Charlotte said.

"What are you saying?" Grace asked.

"Oh, Gracie," Nicole said. "I'm afraid to ask you this, but . . ."

"What?" Grace asked.

"Are you the one who messed up Fanny's posters?" Nicole finished.

Grace was silent for a minute. She looked everywhere but at the other Roses. Finally, she took an enormous breath and sighed loudly. "Okay, yes. I admit it, I taped those things to her posters. I just couldn't stand her attitude! I don't know who she thinks she is, but Nicole would be twice the president Fanny could ever hope to be. It's not fair for her to tell lies and make people think bad things about Nicole!"

"It's not nice, Grace," Nicole said. "You're right.

But that doesn't mean we should stoop to her level."

"I'm sorry, " Grace said. "I guess I didn't think of it that way. I'm sorry that I lost my cool, and I'm sorry that you're all cleaning up the mess I made."

"Our Grace is very competitive!" Binah noted.

"Not being able to play must be driving you crazy!" Nicole said.

"Yeah," observed Charlotte. "It's almost as if you have exchanged the football field for the election arena."

"Which is just fine," Amy said, "as long as you realize that there are rules and penalties in elections, too!"

"Yeah," agreed Nicole. "And the teachers are the referees!"

"I think I just earned my first yellow card," Grace said sheepishly. For those of you, like Charlotte, who have no idea what that means: a yellow card is a warning in football. Get too many of them, and you're out of the game!

CHAPTER 9

# What Else Could Go Wrong?

yellow card #1

Just then the bell rang and the hallways
swarmed with students. As the Roses
pulled the trash bags toward the janitor's
closet, none of them could escape the
feeling that the students hurrying around them
were a little less friendly. No one called out to wish
Nicole luck. No one asked about her election plans.

The school atmosphere seemed much different from yesterday afternoon, before Fanny's posters were ruined. And speaking of Fanny, just as the Roses finished cleaning up, she went sailing down the hallway past them, with Alexis in tow.

"Got any more dirty tricks up your sleeve?" she called to Nicole just loud enough for the students around them to overhear. Several of them snickered and shot disgusted looks at Nicole and the other Roses.

"Certainly not," Nicole answered calmly. "I had nothing to do with your posters being ruined, Fanny. I'm very sorry that it happened."

"Sure, sure," Fanny said dismissively. "The election is tomorrow, and then we'll know that Hampstead students want honest representation. They don't want a president who fights dirty."

Grace glowered at Fanny but said nothing. Then, as Binah couldn't help but notice, a tiny, secret smile appeared on her face. Binah wondered what might be going on in Grace's mind. Before she could ask Grace anything, though, that annoying school bell rang. This one signaled that the girls were about to be late, so they hurried into class. As they settled at their desks, each couldn't help but sigh deeply. What more could possibly go wrong?

I don't want to sound like a broken record, but when you ask yourself a question like that, you've got to be prepared for the answer. What else could go wrong, indeed? Here it comes.

*Thumbs-up for Nikki!*

Longstanding Hampstead tradition held that Principal Turvey made official announcements over the PA during the last period of the day. The announcements included things such as reminders for club meetings, results of various athletic events, and requests to check the lost-and-found box.

The PA system began to crackle, and Principal Turvey's voice boomed through the classroom. He began by listing all of the club meetings to be held immediately after school. Next he began reading off general school announcements. And this is where things get funky. The students had heard these announcements so many times that, at this point, they were only half listening. Principal Turvey had announced these things so many times

that you could hear the boredom in his voice. He always pepped up again for the sports scores part of the announcements, but right now he was lost in the every day; his voice was flat and without inflection. Which is probably why what happened next happened.

It was the strangest thing. After asking students to bring in canned goods for the community food pantry, this is what came out of the room's loudspeaker, in—unmistakably—Principal Turvey's voice: "For the good of the school, you must vote for Nicole Rissman tomorrow. This is very important. Fanny Kingsbury would make a terrible president. Vote Rissman!"

What?!

Suddenly, Principal Turvey seemed to realize what had happened. The PA system abruptly clicked off. There was silence from the speaker box. There was silence in Mrs. Moss's room. No one knew what to do. Nicole was mortified, but then she was stunned when she looked over at Grace. Grace had an enormous smile on her face and gave Nicole a thumbs-up.

Nicole could feel her face burning. Some of the students sitting nearby looked at her oddly. Mrs. Moss looked confused. Charlotte, Amy, and Binah looked concerned. What had Grace done? Was Nicole in on this?

Here's what Grace had done, as everyone found out the next day: She'd snuck into the principal's

office just after lunch, as students were headed out to recess. Most of the office staff was away at lunch themselves. She'd rifled through the pile of announcements from which he read, and she'd slipped in a piece of paper with the announcement endorsing Nicole. She'd bet on the fact that Principal Turvey simply plowed through the everyday announcements; that he wouldn't even notice the extra slip of paper.

1    2    3

Well, she'd won her bet; he'd done exactly as Grace had hoped. Grace felt victorious. Nicole, not so much. Grace sat there proudly, but Nicole couldn't help but read the expressions on other students' faces. First the posters and now this?! Hijacking the announcements was a new low for her campaign!

With a sob, she grabbed her jacket and school bag and ran from the room. She could hear the other Roses calling after her; and, over their voices,

Mrs. Moss herself was commanding her to stop. Although Nicole had never disobeyed a teacher before, she couldn't stop herself. She ran through the hallway, rushing toward the door, any door, to the outside. She had to get out of that school. She had to get away from the mess that was her election campaign. What had happened? She'd had such good intentions. She wanted to make things better for her fellow students. She'd wanted to run a fair campaign. She'd wanted to improve things at Hampstead, and now it was all a big mess!

Nicole ran and ran. She burst through the double doors leading to the street and headed for home. Almost before she knew it, she was sprinting up the front walk of her house. She banged on the front door, too upset to look for her house key.

When a startled Mrs. Rissman opened it, Nicole could hardly speak.

"Mom!" she sobbed as she flung herself into her very surprised mother's arms.

# CHAPTER 10

# Every Vote Counts

I'm not going to kid you. Nicole was in big trouble. Her election campaign was in ruins, and she felt worse than terrible. As big as Nicole's troubles were, though, Grace's were even bigger. While Nicole's flight broke more school rules than she ever dreamed existed, Grace was facing her own music in Principal Turvey's office. Consumed with guilt, Grace had turned herself in. And as Nicole sobbed out the whole story to her sympathetic mother, Grace was facing a very different, very unsympathetic audience at school.

When the final bell rang, the other Roses silently gathered up their books and supplies and headed out to look for Royston. Mercifully, the other students left them alone. Binah noted, much later, that it had seemed as though the three of them had a protective bubble around them. The crowds of students parted to let Binah, Amy, and Charlotte through. By unspoken agreement, the Roses ended up at Charlotte's house, where they tried to enjoy some fresh-baked brownies. Charlotte called both Nicole's house and Grace's house, but no one answered at either place.

Protective

Bubble

While the three Roses were trying to understand what had happened to Grace and Nicole, the
two friends were coming face-to-face at school.
Principal Turvey had called Mrs. Harrison, asking
her to join them at school. Mrs. Kissman, one
smart cookie, had escorted Nicole back to school to
"face the music," "have an intelligent discussion,"
"make things right," and other parental-sounding

things like that. As soon as Grace saw Nicole, she started to cry.

"Oh, Nikki! I'm so sorry!" she said, over and over again.

You may think that Nicole was furious with Grace and screamed at her. You can be forgiven for thinking that, because that would seem a normal, human reaction. You have forgotten, however, with whom you are dealing. When I said that the

Smart cookie

Roses are all for one and one for all, I wasn't kidding. Bad as this rift may appear to you and to me, it was nothing for the Roses. After just the teeniest, slightest, we're-still-best-friends-for-life hesitation, Nicole reached out to hug Grace.

Mrs. Harrison and Mrs. Rissman exchanged worried glances over their daughters' heads. When they saw Fanny and Alexis walk in, both as white as sheets, they were even more confused. What on earth had happened?

Now the thing about adults is, as much as they often seem clueless and confused, sometimes—working together—they can come up with good ideas. This is what happened in Principal Turvey's office on that dreary Thursday afternoon. At the mums' and principal's urging, Nicole and Grace sat

down, face-to-face, with Fanny and Alexis. The adults perched on chairs in the background, content, for the most part, simply to listen to the girls' discussion.

Nicole spoke first. "Fanny, I'm so sorry that the campaign has turned out this way."

"It's my fault!" Grace said immediately. "Nicole told me that she wanted this to be a fair election. I heard her say the words, but I guess I just didn't understand."

"I didn't appreciate you ruining our posters!" Alexis said.

"That's okay, Alexis," Fanny said. "I wasn't exactly playing nicely myself."

"I really, really wanted Nicole to win," Grace said to Fanny.

"And I really, really want to win," Fanny answered. "It would be so cool to be president!"

"I know; I think so, too!" Nicole laughed.

"What should we do?" Grace asked. "The elections are tomorrow!"

"I have a thought," Nicole said. "I don't know what Principal Turvey will think . . . "

"Go ahead, Nicole," the principal said. "The democratic process is all about listening to every voice. That's why it's so important to run a clean and honest campaign. I'm ready to hear a good idea!"

"What do you suggest?" Fanny asked.

Nicole quickly described her plan. Fanny offered some suggestions, too. As Grace watched Nicole lead their little group, she couldn't help feeling (again) what a wonderful president Nicole would make. She was polite and kind and fair. She listened—really listened—to people. Grace hoped she hadn't ruined Nicole's chances forever!

When the janitor pushed his giant broom through the hallways later that afternoon, he was startled by the sight of the three adults and four

girls huddled together, deep in conversation. As Principal Turvey made very clear, democracy isn't always easy, but it's better than the alternatives!

So this is what happened on the next day, Friday. Election day.

Binah, Charlotte, and Amy were very, very relieved to meet Grace and Nicole at their usual spots along the way to school. The girls were dying of curiosity, but they patiently allowed Grace and Nicole to explain the plan to them. Once clear on the details, the five girls linked arms and skipped up to the school doorway.

Which brings us to the school auditorium, the election, and The Big Plan. Students were expecting to hear election speeches from Fanny and Nicole. Instead, Principal Turvey introduced Grace. She looked tiny up there on the podium, blinking in the bright footlights, but her voice was clear and strong.

"My name is Grace Harrison," she began. "I was Nicole Rissman's campaign manager."

"Still are!" Nicole called out from her seat, smiling up at her friend.

Grace grinned back and then continued, "I know, as many of you do, that Nicole would make a fantastic president. She is sincere and honest and

she really wants to help Hampstead. As her campaign manager, I lost sight of the big picture. I was
so focused on trying to destroy her competitor,
Fanny Kingsbury, that I forgot to think about what
Nicole wanted. I ruined Fanny's posters. . . ."

GASP!!!

There was a gasp from the audience at this.

"And I snuck an endorsement of Nicole into Principal Turvey's announcements."

Another gasp from the assembly.

"I'm very sorry for what I did. It wasn't nice and wasn't in the true spirit of democracy. More important, to me, it wasn't what Nicole wanted. I hope that when you vote, you won't hold my actions against Nicole. Thank you."

With that, Grace stepped down from the stage and rejoined the other English Roses. At first, just a few students clapped; but the wave caught, and

soon the whole auditorium was clapping and cheering for Grace. As she looked around the auditorium, Binah saw other students smiling and nodding. It seemed as though Grace had helped to shore up the other students' trust in Nicole.

Needless to say, Nicole's own speech was extremely well received. After an introduction by the principal, Nicole began:

"My name is Nicole Rissman, and I would like to be your student body president. Being president would not be an easy job, but I think I am up for the challenge. I am not afraid to work hard and will represent all students. My platform is simple: I want to make life better here, both inside our school building and outside. I propose a homework help center, where older students could help tutor younger students. I would like us all to work on keeping the school cleaner." This brought a slight groan from the audience. "I would like to see us do more community service, so that we can help those in need. Finally, I don't see why we can't have a Friday afternoon pizza party or ice cream social . . . every week." This brought cheers. "My name is

Nicole Rissman, and I hope you will elect me your next student body president!"

Without any prompting whatsoever from any of the Roses (you have my word on that!), some boys at the back of the auditorium started chanting "Rissman, Rissman, Rissman" as Nicole finished. She rejoined her friends looking happy and nervous, but very, very relieved.

It was difficult for Fanny to follow that, but to her credit, she did get up and give her own speech. She seemed very nervous and anxious to get off the stage.

"My name is Fanny Kingsbury, and I know I'd be the best student body president ever. I have lots of great ideas for our school. If you vote for me, I'll work on getting rid of homework on Fridays and tests on Mondays. I'll even talk to Mr. Turvey about extra social time during class. Thank you!"

To the Roses, it was as plain as the noses on their faces that Fanny didn't even have a platform. Unlike Nicole's plan, Fanny's ideas seemed unrealistic and unlikely to change anything. Who would the students choose?

Actual voting was held as soon as everyone

returned to their classrooms. When Principal Turvey clicked on the PA during last period, he announced that Nicole had won the day. (Secretly, some students were hoping for more bogus announcements, but we won't even discuss that here!) Fanny and Alexis were gracious enough to offer their congratulations to Nicole as she headed down the hall, surrounded by the other Roses.

"Wow, Nikki, we are so proud of you!" said Charlotte.

"We knew you could do it," Binah told her loyally.

Miss Fluffernutter stopped the girls as they passed by her doorway. "Wonderful job, Nicole," she said. "I know that you are going to make a magnificent president. Hampstead is in good hands!"

"Thank you, Miss Fluffernutter," Nicole said.

"I'll see you later, Binah," Miss Fluffernutter said with a wink at the blonde girl.

"Yes, Miss Fluffernutter," Binah said sweetly, with her own wink right back.

As the girls headed outside to where Royston waited to whisk them to Charlotte's house (every election needs a victory party, doesn't it?), Nicole told Grace, "Despite everything, Grace, I am very grateful to you."

"Thank you, Nicole," Grace replied. "I'm so glad I didn't ruin everything for you!"

"Now I've got to figure out cabinet positions for all of the Roses," Nicole confided to her friends.

"Ooops! I think you'd better count me out, Nikki!" Grace said. "From now on, I'm steering clear of politics."

"But you can't, Grace!" Nicole exclaimed. "I've got something special in mind for you. How about Chief Motivator?"

"That's perfect!" Grace beamed. "I am happy to be of service. But you must each promise me one thing."

"What's that, Grace?" Nicole asked.

"I am strictly behind the scenes from now on. I'm saving the Harrison competitive streak for the football field!" Grace laughed.

"Agreed!" the Roses replied as one.

The End

MADONNA was born in Bay City, Michigan, and now lives in New York and Los Angeles with her children, Lola, Rocco, and David. She has recorded 18 albums and appeared in 18 movies. This is the tenth in her series of chapter books. She has also written six picture books for children, starting with the international bestseller *The English Roses*, which was released in 40 languages and more than 100 countries.

JEFFREY FULVIMARI was born in Akron, Ohio. He started coloring when he was two, and has never stopped. Soon after graduating from The Cooper Union in New York City, he began drawing for magazines and television commercials around the globe. He currently lives in a log cabin in upstate New York, and is happiest when surrounded by stacks of paper and magic markers.

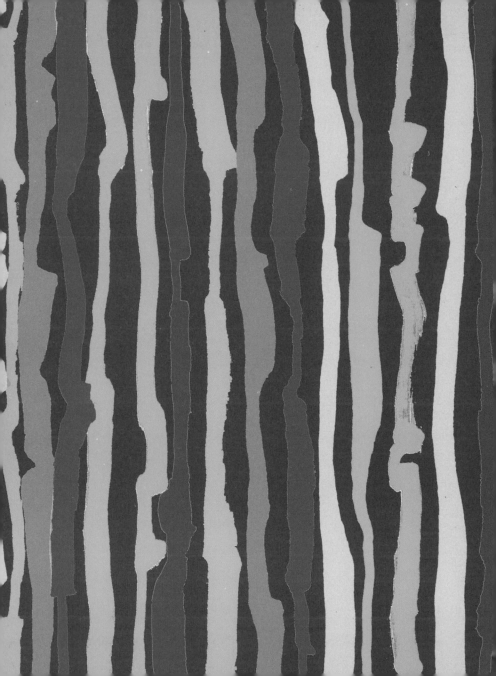